Daddy's Heaven Birthday

Written by Megan Pecoraro-McCann

Illustrated by Elena Delzer

Dedication

For Joe: I will continue to teach your children about how wonderful you are, for the rest of my days on Earth, until I join you for eternity in Heaven. I kiss on it. -Kurtz

For Leo and Belle: May you both always continue to find joy at the center of all you do, despite any tragedy or hardship that comes your way. -Mom

For Ryan: Thank you for supporting this widow through the good, the bad, the beautiful, and the ugly days of grief. I love you with all of me, in this world and the next. -Pec

For Tash: You are one of the three greatest gifts that I've ever received; all because I chose to keep moving forward and focus my life around my ability to love, love, and love some more. -Mommy

For Kathleen Tieri Ton: I dedicate this book to you, who gave me so many opportunities in the arts, including illustrating this book! -Elena

Today is my Daddy's Heaven Birthday.
A year ago my daddy died and went to heaven.

So today is his Heaven Birthday.
That's what I told Mommy.

Today my mom, baby sister, and I
will celebrate the day Daddy went to heaven.

There will be lots of other family and friends who will
be with us to remember my daddy.

One day my mommy told me that
Daddy went to heaven and couldn't be with us anymore.
My daddy's heart didn't work anymore.

That meant that he would go to heaven to be with God.
So all of the things I was starting to learn to do
couldn't be with Daddy anymore.

I miss my daddy so much.
But Mommy and his family and friends help me
so I will never forget him.

They tell me stories about my daddy.
Sometimes the stories make me sad, but most of the time
I smile and laugh. My daddy's the best!

This year was pretty confusing.

me + Dad

I was getting bigger and that meant my daddy and I could start doing lots of things, like playing catch and going to baseball games and getting ice cream cones, just the two of us. Mommy would stay home and take care of my baby sister.

My family did lots of fun things together,
even though daddy couldn't be with us.
We had ice cream picnics at the cemetery to be by him,
and I found my own tree hideout there, too.

Mommy had the best birthday party for me
and so many people came.
I really had a ton of fun!

When I am lonely for my daddy—
sometimes I just cuddle with Mommy.

Sometimes I look at pictures and videos of Daddy.
And sometimes Mommy will tell me a story about Daddy.
That helps me not be so sad and lonely.

I am telling my little sister these stories and showing her the
pictures of Daddy so she will know him better.
It's a really important job for me to teach her!

Today my family will eat pistachio cake and bacon cheeseburgers for my daddy's first Heaven Birthday because mommy told me those are his favorites.

Mommy says I am big enough to blow out the candle for Daddy. I can't wait to hear more stories about him today.

People always tell me my eyes look just like my daddy's.
How cool is that?

The name of the person I love who is in Heaven is: _____

My loved one's Heaven Birthday is: _____

Some words my friends and family use to describe my loved one include:

_____

A way I would like to remember my loved one is:

_____

If I had the important job to teach someone about my loved one, I would teach them about.....

_____

When I feel strong emotions about death or grief, I could talk about it to adults who love me!
Someone I can talk to is:

_____

Grief often feels like a big, giant emotion mixed up of lots of different feelings together!

Use this space to name or draw some of the feelings you have about your loved one's Heaven Birthday.

Use this space to write or draw some stories or memories that make you smile and laugh about your loved one in heaven.

Be creative! Use this area to do whatever makes you smile.

Acknowledgments

To Louise VonHoff: Thank you for encouraging me, over and over throughout the years, to write this book from my son's point of view.

To Elena Delzer: Thank you for your wonderful illustrations of this book. You took my words and put them into beautiful illustrations to bring the emotion to life!

To Kathleen Tieri Ton: Thank you for connecting me to Elena and taking the time to teach me how to publish my work. You are a wonderful, caring, and thoughtful colleague. I am so happy to have worked with you in both a professional and personal way.

To the widows who came before me: Thank you all for sharing your stories and inspiring me to continue living my life to its fullest, despite my intense feelings of grief.

To the widows who will come after me: May you always know you are not alone; sadly, others have walked this walk before you – and we shall be here to help lead your way.

About the Author

Megan Pecoraro-McCann is a Licensed Clinical Social Worker, Certified Clinical Trauma Professional, and Certified Grief Informed Professional. She works as a school social worker at a public school district in the Northwest Suburbs of Chicago and works at a mental health clinic part time doing community outreach programs for youth and families. More than any professional job, Megan considers her role as a wife and mother to be of utmost importance.

Megan and her high school sweetheart, Joe, were together for 13 years when he died suddenly at the age of 28. Their son, Leonardo, was 2 and a half years old and their daughter, Isabelle, was 10 weeks old.

Navigating a new life ahead of her that she never dreamed she would have, Megan relied on her faith in God as well as support from her loved ones, colleagues, therapist, and other widows she met in a local support group to build a new and unexpected life.

Megan fell in love again and married her second husband, Ryan. Together they have a son, Tash.

In her spare time, Megan enjoys crafting as a hobby; this includes scrapbooking, making wreaths, jewelry, and crocheting. Megan is a strong advocate of yoga and mindfulness for people to find a sense of peace and grounding in a world that often feels much out of human control.